This book belongs to:

In memory of my **parents, sister, and brother-in-law**; who taught me to chase after my dreams, to be prepared for the obstacles that my dreams will bring, but most importantly, to keep pushing when those obstacles arise.

terysa solves it
TO THE MOON!

by terysa ridgeway

illustrated by maria gabriela gama

Guess what? It's science fair time.

This is my favorite time of the school year, and I am super excited.

I only have one teensy little problem: how will I decide what to present? I have so many cool ideas. It's hard to choose just one.

"Well, what are you interested in?", Shana asked.

"I have the perfect idea, have you heard of **Dorothy Vaughan's work at NASA?**" my sister Shana asks me.

"Dorothy Vaughan was the space agencies' first-ever Black supervisor. There's even a crater on the moon named after her."

"That's AMAZING!", I exclaimed. I definitely
want my project to be related to Dorothy Vaughan now.
Maybe we can make a rover!

I start off by making a model of the rocket used in the USA's first **orbital spaceflight**, which Dorothy Vaughan worked on, and a model of a **lunar rover**.

Next, I try making a model of the far side of the moon, showing the Vaughan crater.

But again, my moon model doesn't do anything.

"These are no good," I say to Shana.
"I'll never win the science fair prize with models
that don't do anything."

"You know, **Dorothy Vaughan also took the lead
in computer programming at NASA**," Shana says.
"She knew how important computers would be, so
she taught other women how to program them."

This gives me the best idea. **"Wouldn't it be so cool if I could program a rover to move around this lunar landscape?"**

"You could use **Python's turtle module** to do that," suggests Shana. "Start your code with 'import turtle' to load the module. We'll pretend the turtle is your lunar rover. Then, you just need to tell it where to go."

I scratch my head. How can I get the turtle to move?

I try **turtle.move** but nothing happens.

Then I try **turtle.forward** but still nothing happens.

"Forward is a long word to type,"
suggests Shana.
"Try abbreviating it with 'fd'.
And you need to tell it how far forward
you want it to go."

So I type **turtle.fd(10)** and hit *run*.

Woohoo! It works! A window pops up with a little arrow on it.

I try: **turtle.fd(100)**

The arrow has moved to the right and drawn a line across the window.

"This is cool!" I say. "But how do I get it to turn?"

```
PYTHON

IMPORT TURTLE
TURTLE.FD(10)
TURTLE.FD(100)
```

TURTLE.PY

I look at my code.
Maybe I need to tell it how far to turn to the right!

I type: **turtle.right(90)**

turtle.fd(100), and hit run.

The arrow travels to the right, turns right 90 degrees,
then travels down.

```
PYTHON
IMPORT TURTLE
TURTLE.FD(10)
TURTLE.FD(100)
TURTLE.RIGHT(90)
TURTLE.FD(100)
```

TURTLE.py

"This is awesome!" I cry.

"Now, all you need is to work out
how exactly you want your rover
to move."

We call in Dad, Mom, and our big sister, Kelia, and
get them to pretend to be the rover.

"Left 90 degrees, now
forward four steps, now
45 degrees to the right!"

Once I'm happy with how the rover should move,
Shana and I type up all the code, save, and compile
it onto the computer I received for my birthday,
which we attached to my lunar rover model.

I hit *run*, and the rover moves around my lunar landscape just like I've programmed it to!

"And the winner of the 75th Annual Science Fair is . . ." Mrs. Boxie pauses.

I'm holding my breath.

"Terysa with her Dorothy Vaughan inspired lunar explorer!"

Mrs. Boxie hands me my prize, which is a telescope.

"I'm going to share this with my sister, Shana. I wouldn't have been able to solve this problem without her!"

Acknowledgements

To my supportive husband and children. Thank you for loving me with more grace than I feel that I deserve, but most importantly thanks for teaching me how to love deeply and forgive effortlessly.

To my sister and brother-in-law. Thank you for showing me how to live life intentionally and purposefully. I promise to keep "living my best life".

To my nephews. I'm beyond proud of what you've been able to accomplish in such a short time, and I can't wait to cheer on your future accomplishments.

To Mrs. Boxie, my 2nd grade teacher and Aunt, for introducing me to the magical world of Science and Math at an early age.

Additionally, a SUPER special thanks to **Maria Gabriel Gama**, my illustrator for helping bring this vision to life, visually. This book would not have been possible without your creativity and insight.

Terysa Ridgeway

author

Terysa Ridgeway is a Technical Program Manager at Google. Before that, Terysa was a rocket scientist developing code for Exoatmospheric Spacecraft! Terysa holds Computer Science and Mathematics degrees from Southern University and A&M College, and was recently accepted into Stanford University's Executive Education LEAD program.

Terysa is inspired to write by her insanely vivid dreams, stories from her children's 'out of this world' imagination, and by seeing brilliant young minds at work.

Terysa lives with her husband and their four children, a creative ten-year-old, a nine-year-old aspiring author and songwriter, an inquisitive three-year-old, and an energetic two-year-old.

Terysa believes that when it comes to learning, with the right support, the sky is the limit!

❶ /terysasolvesit ⓘ /terysasolvesit
terysasolvesit.com

Maria Gabriela

illustrator

Maria Gabriela Gama is a designer and illustrator from Brazil. In 2019 she obtained a Bachelor's degree in Graphic Design at São Paulo State University (UNESP). Since she was a child, Maria always had a pencil in her hand, ready to draw! So, she opted for a degree in Design and, throughout college, she discovered that it was possible to turn her passion for drawing into her profession. That's when Maria came across the fantastic world of children's illustration and decided to make that dream come true.

She started her professional career working with graphic design in advertising agencies and, today, after graduating, she became a freelance illustrator. Maria works mainly with the children's publishing market and aims to provide joy, representation and positive change through her art.

/mabi.gabi
mariagabrielaart.com

Title **Terysa Solves It: To The Moon**
Author **Terysa Ridgeway**
Illustrator **Maria Gabriela Gama**
Layout Designer **Maria Gabriela Gama**

ISBN 979-8-9850967-6-7 (Paperback)
Library of Congress Control Number: 2022907318
First paperback edition July 2022.
www.terysasolvesit.com

_ □ ×

What Did You Think of *To The Moon?*

amazon

I know you could have picked any number of books to read, but you picked mine and for that I am extremely grateful.

If you enjoyed this book I'd like to hear from you and hope that you could take some time to post a review on Amazon.

Reviews are essential for new book releases and I truly enjoy reading each and every one of them.

You can follow this link to review *To The Moon:*

amazon.com/author/terysaridgeway

Printed in Poland
by Amazon Fulfillment
Poland Sp. z o.o., Wrocław

17169212R00016